With special thanks to Adrian Bott.

# EGMONT
*We bring stories to life*

First published in Great Britain 2015 by Egmont UK Limited
The Yellow Building, 1 Nicholas Road, London W11 4AN

Cover illustration by Jacopo Camagni
Inside illustrations by Artful Doodlers
Text & illustrations copyright © 2015 Imangi Studios, LLC

ISBN 978 1 4052 7633 7

www.ImangiStudios.com
www.Egmont.co.uk

59564/1

A CIP catalogue record for this title is available from the British Library.

Printed and bound in Great Britain by the CPI Group.

MIX
Paper
FSC   FSC® C018306

EGMONT

Y ou're standing all alone in an empty railway station in Ireland, in the middle of the countryside. The train that brought you here has left, and nobody got off here but you. There must be lonelier places in the world than this, but not many.

Eventually a car comes to collect you from the station. The skies overhead are dark and full of storm clouds. As you watch the countryside go by, heading further and further from civilization, you begin to feel like you are in some spooky old movie. It's creepy but exciting at the same time, especially when you think about why you're here.

You check your pockets just to make sure the invitation's still there. You can't resist taking it out and reading it over again.

My young friend,

I see you have been having quite a bit of luck treasure hunting lately. Like so many other people, I watched you on the news when the Cromachie Hoard was uncovered. What an achievement for you to have found such a treasure, and with only a metal detector! How excited you must have been when those few Viking coins you found turned out to be part of the biggest haul of Dark Ages gold ever discovered.

Well done for notifying the proper authorities, too. Now the Cromachie Hoard will end up in a museum where everyone will be able to enjoy it, instead of becoming part of some rich man's private collection. The treasure hunting community needs more young people like you.

Permit me to introduce myself. My name is Philip Appleton, and I was once a treasure hunter like you, though I am too old for such adventures now.

I hereby invite you to spend a spooky weekend at Castle Gloomgarret in Ireland, all expenses paid, for the treasure hunt of a lifetime! This castle is packed with rare, exotic treasures, and I need the help of young people like you to find them.

To add to the fun, there will be two teams. You're the captain of the Red Team. I've hand-picked some famous treasure hunters to join your side. But watch out – there are experts on the Blue Team too.

Hope to see you soon. May the best team win!

When you see Castle Gloomgarret looming on the horizon, you wonder what you've let yourself in for. It's a haunted-looking place, with battlements and towers, and a door like a great gaping mouth. The driver leaves you in the courtyard and drives off without a word. Strange. You shrug and head inside.

There's no sign of this Philip Appleton character, but waiting on a red sofa are three unusual people: a stubbly American with a big grin, an Englishwoman with red hair, and a well-dressed fellow with a pointy beard and a Spanish accent. You glance at the blue sofa opposite, but there's nobody sitting there yet.

'Ah! You must be our team captain,' the Englishwoman says. 'I'm Scarlett Fox. This is Guy Dangerous, and this is Francisco Montoya. Care for some tea?'

'Or beef jerky?' says Guy, taking a strip of something dark out of his jacket. It looks like it's been there for months.

'You three are all on Red Team?' you ask excitedly.

'Indeed,' says Francisco, looking you up and down. 'You seem a little young to be a leader. I hope you will not slow us down. We are all professionals.'

'Charming,' says Scarlett, rolling her eyes. 'Don't worry,' she says to you. 'I'm sure you'll do fine.'

'Don't you know who this is, Francisco?' Guy says. 'This is the kid who found the Cromachie Hoard! We're teamed up with a celebrity here, you goofball! Show some respect.'

Francisco stands up and gives you a stiff bow. 'I apologise. I am a little behind on the news. I do not watch television.'

'He's old-fashioned like that,' Scarlett says, and gives you a wink.

'Well, I'll do my best,' you promise. 'So who's on the Blue Team?'

Guy shrugs. 'Someone we know, Appleton says. I hope it's not Karma Lee. Wouldn't want to be up against that lady.'

As you're settling in, wondering when your host is going to put in an appearance, a boom of thunder resounds through the castle. In strides a tall cloaked figure, followed by two shifty-looking men and a scowling woman. Your team jump to their feet.

'Pedro Silva,' says Francisco, with a hiss like spitting bacon in a pan. 'I never expected to see you again.

Not after you left me trapped in that silver mine in Brazil with nothing to eat but popping candy!'

'Relax!' says Silva. He settles himself on the sofa opposite yours and smirks. 'Is this any way to greet an old friend, hey?'

'You're no friend of ours, you snake,' snarls Guy.

Scarlett adds, 'You've betrayed every one of us at some time or another. '

You get the feeling that Silva's crowd are bad news. The rest of your team clearly have history with him. What on earth have you let yourself in for?

Suddenly Silva glances at you and scowls. 'YOU!'

'Me?' you reply, confused.

'The thief! The one who robbed me of my rightful prize!'

You're not sure whether to be offended, angry or sarcastic, or all three at once. 'I'm no thief,' you yell at him.

'I can explain,' says Francisco, stroking his beard. 'Poor Pedro Silva had been looking for the Cromachie Hoard for years. Then you dug it up before he could.'

'A mere amateur!' rages Silva. 'With a . . . a metal detector! That treasure should have been mine.'

'That treasure is in a museum where it belongs,' Guy says in a warning tone. 'The kid did good.'

Scarlett fingers a teaspoon as if she's about to use it as a deadly weapon. (And for all you know, she can.) 'So, what are you doing here, Silva?'

Silva calms down a little, though he's still giving you poisonous looks that seem to threaten revenge. 'I was invited, same as you. I am the Blue Team captain.'

Guy snorts. 'So we've got two teams who hate each other. I guess that's our host's idea of a fun time.'

'That was the general idea, yes,' says a voice from the hall.

Everyone turns to look, and you get your first glimpse of Philip Appleton. He's a white-haired, jolly old gent who walks with a cane. Scarlett runs up and hugs him like an old friend.

'Why don't you all come through to the dining hall?' Philip says. 'There's a lot of explaining to do, and then the hunt can begin.'

Over a delicious meal of venison and winter vegetables, during which you're served glasses of juice that looks exactly like wine, Philip tells you why you're here. He explains that he's only just bought this castle, using the money he's made from a lifetime of professional treasure hunting. The castle is something of a legend. The previous owner, Sir Barnaby Fleming-Burke, was – to put it mildly – eccentric. He was a famous explorer, and stuffed the house full of artifacts and precious objects from all over the world, as well as strange and exotic creatures nobody had ever seen before. He also fitted the house with all sorts of tricks and traps, such was his fear of being robbed.

Philip is keen for the castle's treasures to be found, especially the most amazing treasure of all, the fabled Golden Idol. But sadly, he says with a shrug, his own treasure-hunting days are behind him. He's just too long in the tooth to go running around in a crumbling old castle, particularly one that's been deliberately fitted with traps! And that's where you young bloods come in.

It's treasure hunt time. Philip's dividing you into two teams: you, Guy, Scarlett and Francisco versus Pedro Silva and his cronies. You have the run of the whole castle, and your mission is simply to gather as many pieces of treasure as you can! Whichever team collects the most treasures will win the contest, and a share of the treasure's value. Philip hands out treasure-hunting sacks: red ones for your team, blue ones for Pedro Silva's.

He also gives both you and Pedro Silva a hand-held device with a little button on it. This, he explains, is the GAME OVER button. If either team captain presses it, the treasure hunt ends – for everyone.

**GAME OVER**

There's a ten minute head start. After that, you can stop the hunt at any time and count up the treasure to see who's won. However, you should probably wait until you've got several treasures before stopping the contest, since the other team might have more than you.

Philip explains that the Golden Idol is so valuable he will count it as FOUR treasures, so finding the idol is likely to be a guaranteed win. However, the stories tell that a fearsome monster guards the idol, the Beast of Castle Gloomgarret. Nobody knows quite what it is, because nobody who has looked upon it has lived to tell the tale. Some say it is a great black dog, others that it's a vast wild boar, and some say it's like no natural animal on earth . . .

'Good luck!' Philip shouts. 'And may the best team win!'

The lights go out. When they flicker back on again, he's vanished. You all look at one another. Philip must have disappeared into a secret passage. Looks like the castle really is riddled with them!

Pedro Silva's team, laughing and mocking, runs off into the castle. 'Amateur,' he sneers, looking right at you. 'You will lose. I will make sure of it.'

Your team has a quick meeting to discuss tactics.

Nobody wants to just sprint off blindly; you need to plan. The castle is vast. It's going to be a challenge to explore. Besides, it's dangerous. Even the moat is full of flying piranhas!

(You're going to need to take notes, because you're starting a treasure-hunting record to keep track of what you find. Note down every piece of treasure you collect. If you don't note it down, you don't get to count it at the end! Don't worry, you'll be told when to write something down. You can use your Treasure Hunter's Log to do this. You'll find it right at the back of this book.)

Guy, Scarlett and Francisco all think you should focus on finding the Golden Idol. You suggest you split the team up, so you can cover more ground. Everyone agrees. However, they all have very different ideas on where the idol might be, and each one wants you to go with them.

Guy thinks you should head up to the castle battlements and rooftops. If the idol hasn't been found in all these years, maybe it's because it's hidden somewhere up high? What better place to hide an idol than among gargoyles and weathercocks? You think he's got a point, but Guy Dangerous's plan sounds, erm, dangerous. And it's looking like there's a proper storm brewing out there. You might slip on the rain-slick stone, or even get struck by lightning.

Scarlett thinks your best bet is to explore the inside of the castle. With so many rooms and doors to choose from, one of them must lead to a treasure room. She's cleverly downloaded a guide to Castle Gloomgarret on her tablet computer. Maybe you can find a map, or some useful information in the library? Besides, castles like these are full of secret passages. You think Scarlett's talking sense, but then, the more rooms you venture into, the more likely it is you'll get completely lost. You don't want to be trapped in a maze of corridors instead of finding the idol.

Francisco thinks the only way to go is down. This place must have cellars, dungeons and tunnels beneath it – they all do! In castles like this, riches are often stored safely in the basement, simply because that's the easiest place to defend. Francisco licks his lips as he tells you about the piles of gold coins just waiting for you to scoop them up. He sounds pretty convincing.

To go upwards with Guy, head to page 14.

To explore with Scarlett, go to page 60.

To zoom downwards with Francisco, turn to page 55.

'I'll go with Guy,' you announce.

'Whoop whoop!' Guy yells, and high-fives you. 'This treasure hunt is as good as won. We'll be back before you know it, with the idol in one hand and a sack of treasure in the other!'

Francisco gives him a sarcastic smile. 'Did you not get a look at the castle from outside, *amigo*? Half the towers are in ruins. You will find nothing up there but bats and spiders!'

'See you later,' Guy says, pulling on his backpack. 'Try not to get trapped in any dungeons.'

Scarlett frowns. 'Look, Guy, I don't want to sound like your mother . . .'

'Then don't,' Guy interrupts.

'. . . but I can't believe you think this is a good idea. In this weather?'

Right on cue, a flash of lightning lights up the windows. Thunder crashes and rattles the china teacups on the table.

'Ah, it's only a spot of rain,' Guy grins. 'Nothing we can't handle. Right, kid?'

'Right,' you say, hoping it's true.

Scarlett sighs. 'Fine. If you fall off the roof and break your legs, don't come running to me!'

It doesn't take long for you to find the way up to the battlements. Guy leads the way, up a spiral stone staircase that twists around and around. At every floor, arrow slits give you a view out over the lands. Archers and crossbowmen must have crouched there once, long ago, carefully taking aim, ready to send some unsuspecting enemy to his grave.

You climb right to the very top and step out on to the battlements through a little wooden door. The dark of evening is made even darker by the storm. Rain is lashing down all around you, spattering your face, soaking your clothes. Guy puts his hands on his hips and grins up at the sky.

'Woo, yeah!' he shouts. 'This is real treasure-hunting weather!'

You can't really agree with Guy on that, so you leave him to it and take your first proper look at your surroundings.

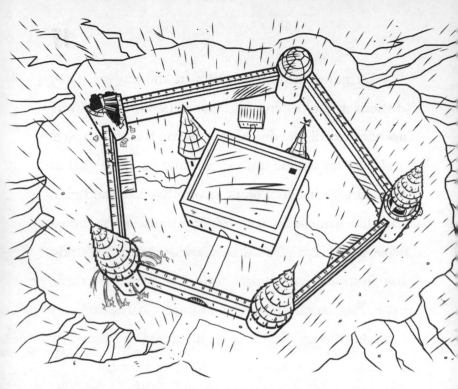

Wow. You're really high up. You can see how the
outer wall of Castle Gloomgarret surrounds the inner
buildings, running around the outside like a great
stone curtain. If you were looking down from above,
it would form a pentagon the size of a football field.
The battlements run along the top of the wall. At
each of the corners of the pentagon, a tower thrusts
up into the stormy sky. You count five in total.

'Look at those towers,' Guy says, sounding smug.
'I bet they're just full of treasure!'

You peer through the rain at the towers. They do look pretty interesting – or dangerous would be another word! The one nearest to you is half collapsed, and you can see the timbers holding up what's left of the staircase inside. The next one has a domed glass roof, like some kind of crazy greenhouse. Then there's what looks like a bell tower, with gargoyles leaning out from it. Next to that a gloomy, dark tower that gives you the creeps just looking at it. The last tower has carved faces on it that spout streams of rainwater down the castle walls in an endless waterfall.

'We can explore them all. Or we can skip a few. Up to you!' Guy slaps you on the back and starts jogging along the battlements towards the nearest tower, the ruined one.

Just then, there's a slow creaking noise. It came from right behind you. You spin around and see a knight in black armour standing outside the doorway you just came out of. It doesn't move. Probably just a suit of armour, you think to yourself. Maybe it was already there. Hard to tell, in this rain.

'Let's get moving,' Guy yells. 'Silva's team might have found some treasure already!'

Side by side, you run towards the ruined tower. The battlements aren't very wide. There's hardly enough room for the two of you to run next to one another. And the rain's making them slippery.

To keep running up to the ruined tower, head to page 31.

To run past the ruined tower and onwards to the greenhouse tower, head to page 93.

You poke the nozzle of the plant food container into the giant flytrap's mouth and begin to pour. It greedily absorbs the liquid. Suddenly it twitches and begins to move.

Guy Dangerous slowly backs away. 'I don't think that was a good idea . . .'

The flytrap bends down towards you. A whispery croak comes out of its mouth: 'More!' As it speaks, you see the object rolling around inside that great green mouth. It's a jewelled egg!

'Hold on just one second,' you tell it. You look around for more plant food, but there isn't any.

'More!' demands the flytrap, sounding really angry now.

Before you can do anything, it lunges for you with its creeper-like arms, draws you in close and snaps you up. Congratulations on your kindness to the environment, but maybe feeding yourself to the plants wasn't the best outcome!

RUN AGAIN? TURN TO PAGE 8

# 20

You leave Scarlett grubbing about in the oven and slip away down the corridor. You find yourself in a gloomy, cheerless room with bunk beds and a single tiny fireplace. This must be where the castle servants lived.

'I could use a little help here!' yells Scarlett. She's a lot less charming when she isn't getting her own way, you think to yourself.

To run and help, head to page 101.

To take a look around first, head to page 94.

You've discovered an amazing and horrible sight. It's a hidden study, with its occupant — now skeletal — still sat at the desk, a quill clasped in his bony fingers. All around you are leather bags that bulge in an exciting way. Weren't there legends of a miserly owner of the castle, bricked up somewhere inside with all his gold?

Scarlett greedily grabs as much as she can carry and urges you to do the same. But you're not sure you should take so much. It could slow you down as you continue on the hunt.

If you want to help yourself to all the gold, go to page 100.

To take only one small bag, head to page 95.

Guy calls out helpful advice to you – 'Put your left foot there, no, there, OK, now your right hand on the ledge' – and you slowly inch your way up the inside of the rain-drenched wall. It's a bit like playing sideways Twister, but you're glad of Guy's help. This would be a lot harder on your own!

Your ten-minute head start is nearly over and you haven't found any treasure yet. You need to hurry. You pull yourself up on to what's left of a wooden platform and try to catch sight of the shiny thing again.

There it is! It's a weathercock on top of the tower, and it looks like it's made of gold. What a find!

But at the worst possible moment, the skies go *skaboom* and a brilliant fork of lightning strikes the tower. Loose masonry falls down all around you. Even worse, the timbers have caught fire! You're trapped halfway up a burning, crumbling tower in a desperate race against time. Mum always said there'd be days like this.

You might be able to reach the weathercock before flames consume the whole tower. Right now they're licking under the support beams for the tower roof. It's up to you.

To climb further up and try to grab the weathercock, scramble on to page 53.

To climb back down and wait to see what happens when the tower roof collapses, retreat to page 30.

To climb back down and run on to the greenhouse tower, go straight to page 93.

You slam the door and quickly heave the bolt shut. It's stiflingly warm in this tower. The plants all around you are colourful and huge.

At the end of the row is something that looks like a gigantic Venus flytrap. It has tentacle-like vines hanging from it.

Its mouth, you are glad to see, is clamped shut, but from between its sharp, pointy teeth comes a silvery gleam. There's something valuable trapped in there. A sign reads 'RARE AND DAINTY EXOTIC BLOSSOM, discovered 1877 by Sir Peregrine Fleming-Burke.'

You have to get the treasure out of that thing's mouth, assuming it *is* treasure. Guy bravely tries to prise the plant creature's jaws apart, but it's no use — they're firmly clamped together. However, he says he can definitely feel a cold metal object in there, with what might be a jewel set into it.

You can see all sorts of gardening implements and bottles of liquid. You can't tell what half of them do, but one seems to be plant food, another weedkiller. Perhaps you could get at the object in the thing's mouth by some other way than brute force . . .

Maybe the plant creature is hungry. You could try feeding it with the plant food, to get it to spit out whatever it's holding as a sort of payment.

Guy's not exactly sure about this. 'It might mutate, or something,' he says, wrinkling his nose.

Perhaps you could try to shrivel the creature up with some weedkiller, so that it will drop whatever it's holding.

Guy likes that plan. 'It's only a plant. It's not like it has any feelings, right?'

But then, maybe going after the thing in the flytrap's mouth is the wrong approach altogether. The earth around the plant creature's roots looks really soft.

**26**

Guy ponders that. 'Objects like the Golden Idol have power, y'know. If it's buried down there, it might be what made this flytrap grow so big.' Plus there's a shovel within easy reach.

If you want to give the creature some plant food, scoot on over to page 19.

To try pouring weedkiller on the plant, head to page 32.

To dig around the roots and see what you turn up, go to page 112.

The next tower is set a little further out than the others, across a sloping rooftop. There's no direct walkway from the battlements to the bell tower. You expect you're meant to get there from the ground. Still, you could cross the rooftop and get to the tower that way, if you were feeling adventurous.

Guy's feeling adventurous. He sets out across the rooftop before you can stop him.

You have the odd feeling you're being watched. You look behind you, and sure enough, a little way away, there's the black suit of armour, still holding the mace! It must be the same one as before. You give it a hard stare. It stands stock still, not moving an inch.

You're just about to turn back to the bell tower when the armoured knight sneezes.

'I knew it!' you yell. 'You *are* following us!'

You hear a muffled curse from whoever's in there. The knight hefts its mace and starts to stride towards you. It doesn't look friendly. In fact, it looks like it wants to play a game of bat and ball. The mace is the bat . . . and you are the ball.

You shout over to Guy Dangerous. 'Guy! There's someone in that suit of armour. I think they're trying to stop us!'

'So get over here!' Guy shouts to you, wobbling on the spot where he's balancing. 'They won't dare follow you in that suit of theirs. Too cumbersome!'

---

Do you climb out across the rooftop after Guy? Then scramble to page 34.

Do you abandon Guy and run on alone? Hotfoot it to page 81.

Or do you run up to the knight and confront them? Page 99 will lead you into battle.

You reach out for the web. Guy yells 'No!' but it's too late. The moment your hand touches it, you're stuck. You try to free yourself using your other hand, but that gets stuck too. The harder you try to get yourself untangled, the more tangled you get. Pretty soon, you're dangling in the middle of the web-strung tower like a bluebottle.

'I told you I didn't need rescuing,' Guy sighs. 'And now we both do. Great.'

'I was just trying to help!' you grumble.

'Aww, I know. You've got a good heart, kid. I respect that. But I think we're out of luck.'

The knight reaches the doorway, looks at you and bursts out laughing. Funny — his voice sounds a lot like Pedro Silva's. The Blue Team must be trying to sabotage you! You're helpless to resist as he cuts the ties that bind you one by one. As he slices the last, you begin to fall . . . You just have time to think, 'This is gonna smart,' before you hit the ground and are knocked unconscious.

**Head to page 116.**

'Ah, clever!' Guy says, approvingly. He knows what you've got in mind. You watch as the fire consumes the support beams below the weathercock.

With a long groan, the conical tower roof falls in. Fragments land next to you with a deafening crash and boom. And there's the weathercock right next to you – a little battered and bent, yes, but still worth a lot of money.

**Note down this treasure: Gold Weathercock.**

'Aww yeah! Our first treasure!' Guy gives you a fistbump and you hurry onwards.

**The next tower awaits – head to page 93.**

This tower is little more than a crumbling shell. A staircase once ran around the inside, but it's mostly collapsed now. Guy slams the door shut behind you. He suggests you move on since the tower looks empty, but then you glimpse a flash of something shiny coming from the very top of the stairs. There's something metallic up there — might it be the idol?

You think you could climb up the stumps of wood and stone where the stairs used to be, but the stones are wet from the rain. Maybe you'd be safer just moving on to the next tower.

---

To climb and try to reach the shiny thing, head upwards to page 22.

To keep running to the next tower, rush to page 93.

The moment you pour the weedkiller on to the flytrap, it growls in fury. The plant rips its rooty legs up out of the ground and lunges at you, trying to gulp you down whole. One of its vine-like arms whips out and winds around your waist.

Luckily, Guy Dangerous is there, machete in hand. He slices the thing's arm off and drags you out

of the greenhouse tower. 'Come on!' he gasps. 'That critter might have friends, and we don't want to hang around and meet them!'

**Run on to page 27.**

Wow, someone stashed an awful lot of armour and junk behind this door. Like, all of it. The moment you open the door, it all topples down on you in a steely avalanche. You're completely buried. By the time you manage to struggle free, you're exhausted. Meanwhile, Francisco has disappeared. He was so obsessed with finding treasure, he didn't even notice you were buried!

You think you can see a second door beyond the heaps of metal junk. You begin to scramble over the mounds of metal – but before you reach the door your feet are tugged away from you and a sack is shoved roughly over your head. In the struggle, you hit your head and black out.

**Head to page 116.**

# 34

You climb over the parapet and follow Guy on to the slippery sloping rooftop. The knight starts to follow, then changes its mind, folds its arms and watches you. Whoever's in that tin can clearly doesn't think it's possible.

Guy is walking straight across the peak of the roof, his arms stretched out like a tightrope walker. 'Best do the same, kid,' he tells you. 'The trick's to get the balance right . . .'

You aren't sure about that. The guttering that runs along the edge of the roof looks strong enough to hold your weight. Maybe you should climb along that instead?

---

To follow in Guy's footsteps, head to page 37.

To climb along the guttering, go to page 126.

Despite Scarlett's warnings, you lift down a heavy crossbow. There's a target on the wall that looks like a fine, erm, target. Your first shot *thunks* right into the bullseye! Before you can cheer, you hear an ominous groaning sound. You and Scarlett stare as a small secret panel swings slowly open in the wall.

You put your hand into the alcove that the panel has revealed and feel around. You draw out an intricately jewelled apple. Looks like you hit the jackpot!

**Note it down in your Treasure Hunter's Log: Jewelled Apple.**

Treasure bagged, you and Scarlett leave the armoury.

But where do you want to head to?

To try the games room, go to page 69.

Or to follow a new lead that Scarlett has found, head to page 82.

Y ou wander through the tunnels under the castle for hours. You're well and truly lost. All these passages look alike to you. But at least you've still got your treasure sack.

Then, up ahead, you see an archway unlike any other. It's encrusted with shells, and a weird glow comes from inside. Heartened, you pick up the pace.

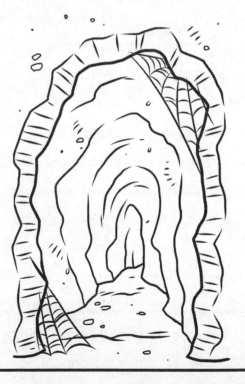

**Hurry on to page 117.**

You take a deep breath and follow Guy out on to the ridge at the top of the sloping roof. With your arms outstretched, you edge towards the bell tower. Something whacks you on the shoulder. You look behind you and see the knight is throwing rocks, trying to knock you off balance! What a jerk.

You can see the bell tower more clearly now. There are four crouching gargoyles around the top. Open arches give you a good view of the bell inside. As you approach, one of the gargoyles' stony heads swivels around and looks at you!

'That's impossible,' Guy gasps. 'Those things are made of solid stone. They can't come to life . . . can they?'

The gargoyle lifts up a metal hammer. You hear a *tick-tick-tick* from inside it as its arm moves. You quickly decide what to do next.

---

To attack the gargoyle from where you are,
go to page 64.

To cross the rest of the distance to the
bell tower and risk being thumped by the
gargoyle, head to page 43.

To think better of it and retreat back to
the parapet, taking your chances with
the knight, scurry away to page 45.

You leap to one side. The monkey, claws outstretched, goes tumbling over the battlements.

Guy whoops in triumph. 'Hoowee! We did it, kid! We got it! We ...'

Guy's grand victory speech dies on his lips as he notices the monkey is hanging on with one claw. It lunges for you with the other. You can't get out of the way fast enough. You're caught up in the monkey's grip and hoisted high above the battlements.

Next moment, the monkey loses its grip on the castle. Holding you in one paw, it falls, howling. You see castle walls zooming past and the greenish-brown water of the moat coming up at you.

*Sploosh!* You're underwater. It's freezing cold, and for a moment you don't know which way is up. But your survival instincts kick in and you struggle to the surface. Miraculously, you're still clutching the idol. Luckily, the demon monkey let go of you when you both fell into the moat. You're amazed to be alive, but there's no time to celebrate. You have to run, and keep running.

You swim to the edge, pull yourself up and out, and start to run again. There's a soggy-sounding roar from behind, and you know the demon monkey hasn't given up either.

**Head to page 57.**

A horrible smell comes from the dark tower. All the windows are boarded up. Whatever's in there must be gross, or dangerous, or both.

Even the knight hesitates, as if it really doesn't want to chase you in there. Perhaps it knows something you don't . . .

But Guy's keen to see what's inside. 'There's gotta be treasure in there.'

'Um, how can you tell?'

'Instinct!' Guy says, ignoring your hesitation. 'There's something epic behind this door. I just know it!' He runs forward and grabs the door handle. 'Pretty please, Team Captain? I need to see what's in here. It feels like my destiny.'

---

**To let Guy have his way and enter the tower, creep to page 51.**

**To keep going to the last of the towers and leave Guy behind, head on to page 54.**

# 42

You lift down *Legends of Gloomgarret*, set it on a desk and look through it.

The book makes your hair stand on end. One chapter describes how one of the owners of the castle in ancient times was a greedy miser who hated to give away anything, however small. Legend has it that his bones still linger deep in the castle, watching over a hoard of treasure gathered in his lifetime. Anyone who finds it must take only a small amount, or risk joining the miser's bones forever.

The illustration on the last page is frightening. It shows a grinning skeleton sitting behind a desk, surrounded by bags of gold. It's very detailed. You get the unpleasant feeling the artist drew the picture from life.

With a shudder, you replace the book and join Scarlett, who thinks she's found a promising clue.

Head to page 82.

With Guy right beside you, you cross the treacherous rooftop and reach the top of the bell tower. The gargoyle draws its arm all the way back, but it doesn't attack you. Instead, it swings the hammer and hits the bell.

# BONGGGGGG!!!

Several deafening bongs later, Guy holds up a finger. 'Oh, I get it. This must be a clock tower.'

You nod and smile. Quick off the mark, that Guy Dangerous . . .

Now you can see under the tower's peaked roof, you realise there's very little to look at. The four gargoyles are ugly, but not very interesting. Even the wooden staircase leading down inside the bell tower has long since fallen away. Below you, the curve of the bell is huge, but it's only dented metal. You can just make out a bellrope dangling there, though. That must be so that people can ring the bell from down below if they want.

'Should we head back?' you suggest.

'Not just yet,' Guy says. 'There's one place we haven't looked. Inside the bell.'

'Inside the bell? How are we going to move it? It must weigh a tonne!'

'No need to move it,' Guy grins. 'Just grab the bellrope and crawl right inside of it. Should be easy. For the, ah, lightest one of the two of us, that is.'

He means you. Well, he is heavier than you are . . . but it's a big risk to ask you to take. Still, the only other option is to head back across the rooftop. You can see the knight looking at you from the battlements, rubbing its gauntleted hands together. You wonder if you'll even make it across the roof, with the knight trying to stop you.

---

**To do as Guy says and grab the bellrope, head to page 103.**

**To head back across the rooftop and try to reach the next tower, head to page 143.**

'You better get out of my way, whoever you are,' you yell to the knight boldly. 'I'm coming through!'

You set out across the roof, hoping to make your way back to the battlements. The knight isn't impressed with your challenge. Worse, it has a big supply of stones to throw at you. You dodge the first two that come hurtling your way, but the third knocks you off balance. You skid down the rooftiles and go plummeting over the edge. The knight punches the air with an iron fist and laughs. What a meanie!

Luckily, you don't fall very far before landing on another section of roof. You go smashing straight through the tiles and land with a whump on a floor of wooden planks.

You're lying on your back in a dusty attic. You're battered and bruised, but not badly hurt. But as your eyes get used to the darkness, you see the rafters are covered with dangling black shapes. Bats! Thousands of them!

An idea comes to you, there in the shadows.

You may have been cast down, but now you will emerge, reborn, as a dark avenger. You will fight crime wherever you find it, and battle the world's most dastardly criminals. All you need is a symbol. You reach out to the bats . . .

Then one of the bats bites you. The treasure hunt gets called off as you are rushed to the hospital for a tetanus shot. No dark avenging for you, unfortunately.

RUN AGAIN? TURN TO PAGE 8

'No! Don't let go! What are you doing? Noooooooooo . . .'

Guy's panicked yells ring in your ears as you drop from the broken guttering into the foul-smelling old stone pipe. There's nothing to stop your fall or even to slow you down. You go shooting into total darkness, sliding on the muck and slime of who knows how many centuries.

What's this stone pipe even for, you wonder? Maybe it's part of the castle's crazy drainage system. You hope you don't splash into a sewer.

Fortunately, the smelly part is soon over and you find yourself shooting down a smooth section of pipe, while white water foams all around you. You're going at a giddying speed. So long as you don't hit anything, you might even have some fun here.

But then you start worrying you'll get trapped in the pipe. Isn't there a children's story where something like that happens to an overweight German kid? It doesn't end well, you know that much.

Luckily, the pipe doesn't get narrower. It gets wider. You hear the squeak and chitter of rats. Then, suddenly, you fly out of the end and plunge into shockingly cold water.

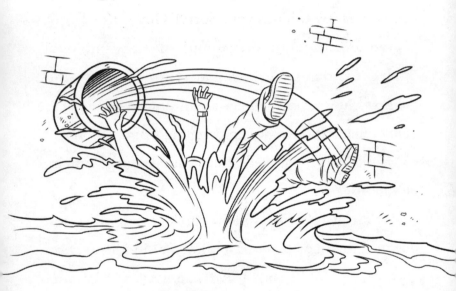

**Splash on over to page 59.**

'Hang in there, kid. I'm coming!'

Your fingers are starting to ache. Guy scrambles across the roof and edges his way down the tiles. His boots dislodge some loose tiles that come rushing towards you. 'Sorry!' Guy yells.

You manage to dodge out of the way, but the guttering is beginning to creak under your weight. Whoever nailed it on obviously wasn't expecting a kid to end up dangling from it.

'Guy, help!' you yell. 'I can't hold on for much longer!'

Guy knows it's his moment to be a hero. You can tell, because he's humming an action movie theme from the 80s. He skids down the last few feet and holds out his hand to you.

'Easy, kiddo. I gotcha.'

Unfortunately, Guy is seconds too late, and he hasn't gotcha. He doesn't get to be a hero today. The gutter snaps off completely, and it takes you with it.

You don't enjoy the experience. You

do bounce off several quite fascinating stone sculptures on the way down, however. Isn't history exciting?

RUN AGAIN? TURN TO PAGE **8**

You try the door, but it's damp and swollen. You can't budge it.

'Never mind, Guy,' you tell him. 'We tried. Let's go, before the knight catches up to us.'

'Oh no. We don't give up that easy. I tell you, kid, this is destiny calling.' Guy puts on his 'macho explorer' face and tells you to stand back. 'There's only one thing to do in these situations,' he explains. He crouches down, mutters something that sounds like '*hut, hut, hut,*' and charges.

He crashes through the door. You hear his scream as he falls over the edge of a pit, then a muffled, 'I'm all right!'

You resist the urge to facepalm.

'You don't need to come in,' Guy yells.

You shake your head and look inside. You don't see him at first. Slowly, you look down . . . and down . . . and down.

Guy is dangling spreadeagled in a huge, sticky web. This tower has no floors at all, it's just a hollow brick cylinder with webs entangling it! You really *don't* want to see the spider that made those.

You glance over your shoulder and see the knight closing in on you.

'Everything's cool,' Guy assures you. 'I know this looks bad, but trust me, I've been in worse. I'll be out of this web quicker than you can say "Tezcatlipoca"! You just head on without me.'

You think quickly. There's a long, ropy strand of web hanging close to you. The spider that span it must be the size of an elephant, but you can't worry about that now. If you tried shimmying down it, you might be able to reach Guy.

Or you could leave Guy to fend for himself, and just keep running to the last tower. It's what he says he wants, after all.

To climb down the web strand, go to page 29.

To keep going to the water-spouting tower, head to page 54.

Your hand closes on the precious golden weathercock. It looks immensely valuable. Unfortunately, your life was a lot more valuable, and you've not looked after it very well! The timbers below you give way and you fall, with half a tonne of rubble falling after you.

It's going to take a lot of work to dig you out. The treasure hunt will be over by the time you are freed from your rubble heap. And you lost the weathercock in the fall. On your next time through, you might have better luck! Run again?

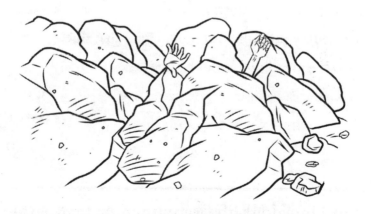

**RUN AGAIN?** TURN TO PAGE **8**

Reluctantly, you leave Guy and run to the last tower. The water spouting from the strange faces you noticed earlier flows into huge ornamental stone channels, which wind around the tower like a helter-skelter. Whoever designed this castle sure had some funny ideas about architecture!

You realise the knight is about to catch you and Guy's not here to help. You could end the treasure hunt now and hope you've got enough treasure to win. One push of the red button, and it'll all be over.

But then you notice a wide metal shield with a leaping fish on it hanging on the wall, and another idea pops into your brain. You could grab that shield, sit on it, and ride down one of the stone channels like a water slide. You have no idea where you'd end up, though!

**GAME OVER**

To hit the GAME OVER button, head to page 145.

To ride the stone channel that vanishes into the darkness of the castle, head to page 59.

You and Francisco set off in search of a downward staircase. You soon find one, a steep, crazily twisting thing with a smooth polished banister. For some reason it's been built in a wide, empty shaft instead of having a nice safe wall around it. Some of the wooden steps look pretty rickety, too. You prod one of them with your foot and it breaks clean in half. The wooden fragments go tumbling silently down into the dark.

You are about to turn back and look for a less deranged way down, when the woman on Pedro Silva's team appears behind you, holding a little cage. The evil grin on her face takes you by surprise. 'Good luck treasure hunting with these little blighters following you around,' she cackles.

She opens the cage and runs away laughing. Out come a horde of bat-winged creatures like golf balls with sharp teeth and single horns. This can't be good.

'Winged Screamers!' shouts Francisco. 'Cover your ears!'

You're furious that the Blue Team is using dirty

tricks to get try to get the upper hand. But there's no time to dwell on it. The swarm of Winged Screamers are heading right for you, shrieking like banshees. You need to get out of there, fast!

'Slide, *amigo*! Down the banister. It's our only hope!' Francisco yells.

To slide down the dangerous-looking banister, go to page 90.

To run down the stairs, go to page 106.

With the Golden Idol under your arm, you run. Nothing seems to matter any more but keeping the idol safe. You wonder if it's got some strange power over you, but it's much too late to do anything about that.

You run through the glorious Irish countryside, over green grassy hills and along the sides of rivers. You run until the sun goes down and the moon comes up, and you keep running until the sun peeps over the horizon once again. You don't seem to need sleep any more. You don't ever get tired. You just run, and run, and run.

The demon monkey is always there, dogging your heels, never quite catching up. There are some close calls when you stumble or trip, or when you blunder through a patch of vegetation and have to slow down for a moment. But you're soon off again, running for your life like you always do.

You sometimes wonder what happened back at Castle Gloomgarret. Did they end the treasure hunt without you? Which team won? It feels like it doesn't really matter now that you've got the idol.

You run and run forever. New legends are told in Ireland, legends of a Running Child and a Demon Monkey who appear out of nowhere and vanish back into the mists. Folk singers make up songs about you, songs which have lots of *tirra-lirra-lirras* in them. At least you've achieved fame, of a sort . . .

**Run to page 57.**

Y ou end up floundering in a stone-lined pool of water, somewhere far below the castle. At least the water is deep – otherwise you'd be strawberry jam by now. Something brushes your foot. You're not sure, but it felt like it could be a tentacle.

You quickly swim to the edge of the pool and climb over.

You just had a lucky escape, you realise. You're wet and shivering, and you're all alone, but you're alive. And you've still got your treasure-hunting sack. Things could be a lot worse.

You shine your pocket torch around the walls and light up the entrance to a tunnel. It's the only way out of here, so you take it. You think about shining the light into the pool, just to see if it *was* a tentacle down there, but then decide you'd rather not know.

**Head onwards to page 116.**

Scarlett's delighted that you have chosen to explore with her. 'Brains over beefcake,' she smirks. 'Let's show them how it's done!'

She knocks back her tea and together you rush out of the great hall. Scarlett quickly pulls up a guide to Castle Gloomgarret on her tablet; it was written in the 1870s, but a lot of it should still be true today, she reckons. According to the guide, there are three impressive rooms on this floor that you should probably investigate: the library, the games room and the armoury. 'What do you think, Team Captain?' she says, an eyebrow raised.

The library might be full of really stuffy old books, but then it might have some awesome ones too, maybe even some with clues in them. You can think of loads of places to hide treasure in a library's dusty corners and crannies.

You're not sure what sort of games will be in an old castle's games room, but you're pretty sure they won't play in HD or use controllers. However, a lot of old-fashioned games are tests of skill, and that sounds like just the sort of thing to unlock a hidden treasure.

The armoury sounds like it'll be full of amazing old weapons. You think about swords with jewelled hilts and shields inlaid with silver. It might be too obvious a place to look, but it could be worth a try?

To visit the library, go to page 62.

To run to the games room, go to page 69.

To explore the armoury, go to page 76.

'Wow,' says Scarlett as you push open the double doors to the library. 'This place could do with a spring clean. Looks like nobody's been in here in years!'

Huge stacks of books loom over you on all sides. Even the support pillars that hold up the roof are fitted with bookcases. The windows have shelves across them, and only let in a tiny amount of light. Some of the book stacks are many times taller than a person, and have sliding ladders built in so you can reach the topmost shelves. The place is so grey with dust that it's like stepping into an old black-and-white photograph.

'OK, well, this could be like looking for a needle in a haystack,' Scarlett says. 'But hopefully we'll find clues the others won't know about.'

'Fingers crossed,' you tell her. 'Let's hit the books!'

But which books do you want to grab and read?

You take a quick look over the shelves and immediately three volumes catch your eye. There's *Legends of Gloomgarret*, *The Treasure Hunter's*

*Handbook*, and a great big old black book with no title. Its spine is covered with creepy symbols, including a skull.

'We can only afford to take five minutes here, then we'll have to move on. Clock's ticking!' says Scarlett.

Choose well!

To read *Legends of Gloomgarret*, scurry along to page 42.

To browse *The Treasure Hunter's Handbook*, head over to page 65.

To delve into the black book with no name, go to page 67.

You charge towards the gargoyle. It stiffly draws back an arm, the hammer clutched in its stony fingers. It must be about to attack you! But you're going to get the first blow in. One good shove should send it over the edge. Then you can watch it smash into little pieces on the ground below.

But the gargoyle doesn't hit you Instead, it uses the hammer to wallop the bell. A deafening *BONG* rings out across the castle. It's OK – it's a clockwork mechanism. The gargoyle is just striking the hour. This must be a clock tower as well as a bell tower!

All of this flashes through your mind in the split-second it takes you to realise – too late! – that the gargoyle wasn't attacking you at all. You try to come to a halt. But you're going too fast and the roof is too slippery. You fly off the edge and out over a very, very long drop.

# WHEEEEE!

**RUN AGAIN?** TURN TO PAGE **8**

You lift down *The Treasure Hunter's Handbook*. For a 'handbook' it's huge, at least three inches thick and as wide as a newspaper. You open it up, wondering what tips the treasure hunters of Victorian times are going to pass down to you.

To your amazement, the pages have been hollowed out. It's not a book at all, it's a cunningly disguised box designed to look like a book! Inside, hidden in a padded cavity, is a brooch in the shape of a four-leaf clover.

You grin to yourself as you lift it into the light. It's solid silver, and worth a whole lot of money. Looking in musty old books proved worthwhile after all! You slip the precious thing into your treasure-hunting sack.

**Add this item to your list: Silver Four-Leaf Clover.**

'Hey, Scarlett?' you call. 'You'll never guess what I've just found! Let's just say I must have the luck of the Irish.'

'I've found another clue, too,' Scarlett says. 'Go team!' You trade a quick high-five.

Where do you want to head now?

---

To follow where Scarlett's clue leads, head to page 82.

Or perhaps you fancy checking out the armoury next. Head to page 76.

Or maybe it's time to search the games room. Head to page 69.

Y ou hesitate before touching the black book. You notice that the spine of the book is in fact decorated to look like a human skeleton's spine. The skull at the top seems to grin at you.

You remember the tales Philip Appleton told about this place. Stories that previous owners of Castle Gloomgarret had some pretty funny hobbies. A few of them were even supposed to be – gulp – dark wizards, calling up the ghosts of the dead. But that can't happen in real life, right?

You pull the book from the shelf. It tilts forward a little way, then with a *click*, a secret panel opens in the wall.

'Scarlett!' you yell. 'Come and take a look at this!'

Scarlett's mouth falls open. 'An actual secret passage in a spooky old castle! How cool is that?'

'I know, right?' You step towards the dark doorway and hold your light up. The opening's draped with cobwebs – old, dusty, undisturbed cobwebs. If you go in, you'll be the first to do so in a long time.

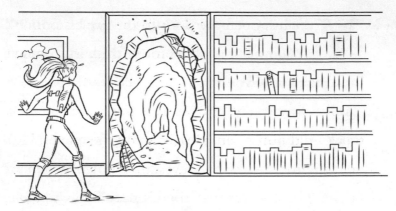

'Careful,' Scarlett warns. 'The secret passages in Gloomgarret are meant to be very dangerous. People have entered them and never returned.'

'But what better place to hide a treasure than a secret passage?' you suggest.

'Hmm. You've got a point. I've found a clue in one of the books, but this tunnel might be better. You're Team Captain. Make the call.'

**If you want to enter the secret passage with Scarlett, head to page 98.**

**If you'd rather follow the clue that she's found, head to page 82.**

Y ou push open the door to the games room.

'Wow. For a games room, this place doesn't look much fun,' you say.

The first thing you see is a huge portrait of a staring old nobleman. He gives you the creeps. He's got sunken cheeks and eyes that bulge like hard boiled eggs. Besides that, there's an old billiard table, a warped dartboard, a rack filled with polo mallets, and – to your disgust – a selection of mounted animal heads running around the top of the room. There's a lioness, a boar, and even something that looks to you like the skull of a monstrous monkey.

'What kind of creature is that?' Scarlett wonders. 'Too big for a mandrill, and it's not a bear.'

At least the trophy cabinet looks interesting. There are cups and statuettes in there. Maybe there's treasure too.

---

**To search the trophy cabinet, head to page 108.**

**To have a closer look at the animal heads, head to page 70.**

You stand on a chair to take a better look at the animal heads. Mostly, they just make you feel sad. Some of these are protected species now. Who could have thought a lion would look better gathering dust up here on a wall than running free on the plains?

You pat the lioness on the nose. Then you notice something strange. She's cross-eyed. It kind of spoils the whole 'noble beast' effect. Who would make a trophy look goofy like that on purpose? Maybe whoever stuffed it was a complete amateur. Or maybe, just maybe, the eye pointing the wrong way is a clue . . .

You know what you have to do. You don't want

to do it, but you take a deep breath and pull the glass
eye out.

'Ew!' yells Scarlett. 'Was that really necessary?'

'I'll know in a second!' you say. You shine your
light inside.

Sure enough, tucked away in the little socket is a
tiny object wrapped in cloth. You pull it out, climb
back down and unwrap it.

Lying in your palm is a beautiful statuette made
from gold and precious stones. She's got a woman's
body and a lion's head. Scarlett gasps. 'It's Sekhmet!
One of the Egyptian warrior goddesses.'

'A treasure?'

'Definitely. And a juicy one, too!'

**Add this to your list of treasures: Egyptian Statuette.**

Just as you're wondering what else there is to explore in here, the eyes on the creepy portrait move. Scarlett sees it too. Like some corny old ghost movie, the eyes are peepholes and there's someone watching you from behind them. It could be one of your friends, like Guy or Francisco, or perhaps Philip Appleton. Or it could be someone from Pedro's team.

Scarlett isn't for taking chances. 'Let's get out of here and try something else! Quick!' she yells. Without waiting for you, she dashes out of the room.

To run out of the room like Scarlett wants, hop over to page 82.

To wait where you are and see what happens next, head straight on to page 73.

'Who's there?' you call.

The eyes blink, but there's no answer.

'Come out where I can see you!' you demand.

Whoever is hiding behind that portrait isn't planning on coming out any time soon. You take a step closer and wonder if you can pull the whole thing down off the wall. That should unmask your mystery observer.

With a *clack,* the painting's mouth opens. A little bamboo pipe pokes out of it.

In that second, you know for sure that whoever's back there wants you out of the treasure hunt. You start to run for the door, but you're just not quick enough.

There's a soft *phut,* and you notice a feathered blow dart sticking out of your chest. Suddenly you feel woozy and drop to the floor. Just before your eyes droop closed, you see the figure of a man standing over you. It's one of Pedro Silva's goons.

'Don't worry,' he says, laughing. 'The poison isn't fatal. But it will send you to sleep . . . for a year or two!' You can still hear him still cackling as he runs out of the room.

You only have a moment to think about what a rotten lot of scoundrels the Blue Team are, before you're well and truly in Dreamland. Let's hope all your dreams are sweet ones – you're going to be asleep for a long time . . .

ZZZZZZZZZZZZZZZZ

**RUN AGAIN?** TURN TO PAGE **8**

Francisco's despairing cry rings in your ears as you defy his advice and head down the right banister. You realise within seconds that you're not hurtling towards a heap of gold. That shimmer you saw was lamplight on water after all. You're about to fly off the end of the banister into a huge underground lake, or pool – you're not sure which. But it's wet.

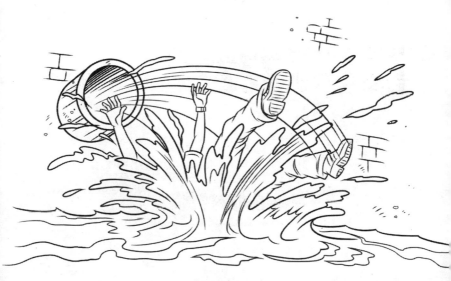

**Shoot onwards to page 59.**

'Now *this* is more like it,' you say as you enter the armoury.

This room is absolutely packed with cool medieval gear – suits of armour, swords, crossbows, maces, all sorts!

'Ooh yes!' grins Scarlett. She knocks on a steel helmet and holds up her fingers in a 'horns' shape. 'Heavy metal!'

The two of you quickly search the room. You find enough armour and weapons to equip your own personal army, but nothing that you could really call treasure.

One of the suits of armour does seem to be missing from its pedestal, though, which is odd. Maybe someone from the enemy team is running around the castle with a suit of armour on. You remind yourself to watch out for crazy knights as you explore.

After ten minutes of searching, Scarlett is all for moving on. 'Let's face it, chum. There's no treasure to be found in here.'

'I dunno,' you say. 'Some of this stuff must be worth a lot of money.'

'Armour and shields are great, yes, but we can't exactly carry them with us, because they weigh a tonne. Let's cut our losses and keep going.'

You don't know if you want to leave just yet. Perhaps you could try out some of the weapons before you go. There's a sword that looks especially cool, with a wavy blade and a long handle, like something out of one of those epic Hollywood movies that always come in three parts. Or maybe you could fire one of the crossbows – they look like they pack a punch.

But maybe you should listen to Scarlett, who is looking at her watch and tapping her foot impatiently.

---

To follow Scarlett out of the room, head over to page 82.

To grab a sword and give it a bit of a swing, go to page 79.

To take down a crossbow and try some target practice, shoot over to page 35.

You reach for the sword. 'I'm just going to have a go with this.'

Scarlett rolls her eyes. 'Fine. But we're using up precious time . . . Captain.'

That woman just likes to suck the joy out of everything. You lift the sword and take a couple of practice swings. It's not as heavy as you expected. In fact, you're pretty sure you could fight with it if you had to. A big grin spreads over your face as you brandish your new weapon.

'Okay, that's enough!' Scarlett warns.

You ignore her. You wonder how it feels to swish your sword in a circle over your head like a barbarian. Wow. It feels good.

Scarlett yells at you to stop, but you're having too much fun. The sword feels amazing in your hands. You slash, thrust, swing – and knock over a suit of armour. It falls into another suit of armour, which falls into another, and so on like dominoes. The sound they make is unbelievable, like an explosion in a dustbin factory. After an agonisingly long time, the toppling stops and you're left standing in a scene of total chaos.

'Oops,' you say.

'We'd better move before Philip finds out what you've done!' snaps Scarlett.

Feeling sheepish, you hang the sword back up on the wall.

**Head to page 82.**

You yell that you're not risking your neck on any stupid roof and that Guy ought to think twice before rushing off. You're meant to be a team!

Guy is so shocked that he climbs back over the parapet and rejoins you. 'Sorry, kid,' he mumbles. 'I guess sometimes I act first and think later, you know? They do call me Dangerous for a reason.'

With the black knight following close on your heels, you run on to the next tower.

**Head to page 41.**

Scarlett thinks you need to be on the other side of the building, in the kitchens. Her research suggests there's a splendid treasure to be found 'in the ashes of a humble fire', and what fire could be humbler than a kitchen's? To get there, you'll just have to dash across the central courtyard.

You both start out across the green lawn, big grins on your faces. But next second, an arrow *thunks* into the ground next to you. You look up and see a hooded figure with a bow. Someone's shooting at you from the battlements!

'Pedro Silva's team, no doubt,' Scarlett snarls, as you retreat back under cover. That makes you mad. You knew they were a bunch of lowlifes, but this is ridiculous.

There's a replica catapult set up on the lawn. If it's in working order, you could use it to shoot back at your attacker just like a medieval warrior.

But how on earth are you gonna be able to get over to it?

One option could be to send Scarlett across
to the catapult, while you distract the
archer by shouting at him. You'd need to
find something to protect yourself with.
To try this, head to page 84.

Or you could just try making a run for it. To
dash across the courtyard as fast as you can,
head to page 89.

If you'd rather forget about Scarlett's plan
to cross the courtyard altogether, you could
always run off into the castle by yourself.
To do that, head to page 97.

You pick up a large shield lying nearby and run out into the courtyard, hoping it's strong enough to stop the arrows flying at you. 'Hey!' you yell. 'Want to try that again?'

Sure enough, the next arrow fired at you ricochets off with a *spanggg*. The archer yells curses at you, sounding remarkably like Pedro Silva. That man just has no sense of fair play!

Next moment, he howls in fear as a rock comes hurtling at him, fired from the replica catapult. You hear stampeding feet and shouting as Silva hurriedly abandons his post.

Scarlett grins at you. 'Teamwork!'

You quickly run the rest of the way across.

**Head to page 87**.

The moment you run in front of the first of the ovens, a huge blast of flame bursts from it. Mmm, crispy explorer! Your adventure is over.

RUN AGAIN? TURN TO PAGE 8

The elevator carriage rumbles down into the darkness once again. Maybe you'll find somewhere to hide from the demon monkey in the depths of the castle.

You freeze. What's that twanging noise? Oh no. It sounds like the demon monkey is biting through the elevator cables.

One moment the carriage is descending slowly. The next, your stomach lurches as it plummets. Sorry to tell you this, but you're shooting downwards at high speed, and you're about to come to an abrupt stop. The result is a bit like being fired from a cannon straight at a brick wall.

If you like, you can pretend that the runaway lift smashes through into a magical cavern full of friendly goblins who welcome you to their tribe. It's nicer than what really happens, that's for sure . . .

RUN AGAIN? TURN TO PAGE 8

You make it to the other side and hastily search for the castle kitchens. On the way, you run through a corridor where the suits of armour swing axes at you! It looks like the whole Blue Team has it in for you. At least by spending so much time sabotaging your team, they can't be discovering many treasures of their own . . .

Eventually you find the kitchens, which are huge, cavernous and stiflingly hot. There are ovens down each side of the room in a line, and they're not just warm, they're belching out flames.

This place is crazy. Even the ovens have been turned into a trap! You really don't want to be roasted alive.

'Ashes of a humble fire,' Scarlett mutters. 'We have to put these flames out if we're going to look inside the ovens.'

You can see a water pump and a bucket, but wouldn't you know it, they're at the far end of the room. If you can reach them you could douse the flames. The question is, how are you going to get past the raging ovens?

Maybe the flames aren't real. They might be some kind of special effect, and you could just run right through them.

Then again, the kitchen floor is kind of greasy. That could work to your advantage! You could do a running skid and slide past all the ovens at once, ducking under the flames.

Then you realise there's a rhythm to the fire-belching. You think you could walk, pause, and walk again. That way, you should avoid the flames.

Or perhaps you think you've already collected enough treasure and you want to end the hunt altogether, before things get even more dangerous?

---

To run through the flames, head to page 85.

To try ducking and skidding, head to page 105.

To walk-pause-walk, head to page 91.

To press the GAME OVER button and end the treasure hunt, head to page 145.

Unfortunately, although you can run fast, you can't outrun an arrow. The good news is that it didn't kill you on the spot; the bad news is that taking an arrow to the leg is no joke. You can't even prove that it was Silva's team who did it, because you didn't get a good look at the archer.

The treasure hunt is cancelled, but Philip Appleton is so upset about your injury that he invites you to spend the whole summer at Gloomgarret with your family, living like a king. You might not have any treasure, but eating feasts every day and going riding in the woods is pretty cool!

**RUN AGAIN?** TURN TO PAGE **8**

Y ou go shooting off down the banister. It's so smooth and polished, you realise it was designed for this purpose. Wow, it must be great to be a crazy old noble with more money than sense. You leave the Winged Screamers flapping helplessly behind you, unable to keep up.

You hold your fist out as you whoosh away from them. *Yeeeeaaaahhhh!* Power slide!

Francisco comes sliding down after you, trying to look dignified and failing completely.

Down below you, the banister splits, along with the stairs. To the left, it curls around and around before vanishing into darkness. To the right, it descends into a steep plunge. You think you see something glittering down there. It's either the gleam of gold, or the reflection of lamplight on a watery surface.

'Go left!' yells Francisco behind you.

To go left, slide to page 107.

To go right, slide to page 75.

'Good luck!' whispers Scarlett.

You carefully count down the seconds between fire blasts and the moment you're sure it's safe, you walk. Flames shoot out behind you, missing you by mere inches. That was too close! Your heart is beating like a samba band, but you keep it together. You use the same method to dodge past the next oven, then the next.

Wearing a smile of victory, you fill up the bucket and chuck water over the flames. Scarlett cheers you on. From somewhere behind the walls, you hear angry voices muttering. Looks like you've thwarted a Blue Team plan to get revenge on you . . . this time, anyway.

Once the smoke and steam have cleared, you

resume your search. Scarlett's convinced the 'humble fire' has to be one of the kitchen ovens, and she wants to look inside every one of them.

'This is going to be a mucky job,' she warns. 'Better roll your sleeves up.'

---

To go and help her look inside, head over to page 96.

Maybe you don't want to rummage through oven muck, though. If you'd rather leave her to it and explore on your own, go to page 20.

This short, stubby tower has a domed glass roof. Inside, you can see the leaves and blooms of enormous exotic plants. Well, Philip did say that the former owner of the castle was a well-known explorer who brought back strange species from all over the world. This must be his plant collection, and by the look of it, it's flourishing.

You're not sure if a greenhouse is the most likely place to find treasure. But then, there's bound to be plenty of soft earth there for the plants. It could be a clever hiding place for a buried idol.

You glance over your shoulder. There's a familiar-looking suit of armour standing just behind you. It's holding a spiky mace in both hands. Is that knight following you? No, it can't be. It must be a different one. A castle like this one must be full of them.

---

To duck into the greenhouse tower, head to page 24.

To keep running until you reach the next tower along, head to page 27.

A thought comes to you. Surely a servant's fire is the humblest fire of all? You dig around in the ashes and soon find a hidden compartment in the stone. You prise it open to reveal a diamond bracelet which must be worth a fortune!

**Note this down in your Treasure Hunter's Log: Diamond Bracelet.**

Scarlett's still yelling for you to come and help. You grin. She doesn't know you've already found the treasure she's looking for!

If you think you've collected enough treasure to win, you can press the GAME OVER button now. To do this, go to page 145.

If you want to go and show Scarlett what you've found, head to page 101.

You take only one bag, and convince grumpy Scarlett to leave hers behind. As you climb out, an iron grate begins to grind across the shaft. The two of you dash for the passage and manage to make it out, but only just.

**Note this down in your Treasure Hunter's Log: Bag of Gold Sovereigns.**

**Run on to page 102.**

Y ou and Scarlett rummage through the gunge in the oven, but find nothing.

'Never mind,' she says. 'It must be in the next one.'

You move on to the next oven. Scarlett shouts in triumph as she holds up . . . a lump of coal. She realises what she's grabbed and sighs. 'Blast. I thought it might be a diamond or something.'

'In a few million years it might be,' you shrug.

After several more minutes of digging through the ashes and finding nothing, you begin to wonder if you're looking in the right place.

Plus you're tired of mucking about in wet ashes, and Scarlett doesn't look like she'll be ready to leave any time soon.

---

**If you think you've collected enough treasure and want to press the GAME OVER button to end the hunt now, go to page 145.**

**Or if you want to leave Scarlett to it and explore on your own, head to page 20.**

You sneak away down draughty corridors, experimentally tugging on candlesticks just in case a secret passage opens. Nothing moves.

Just as you're turning a corner, rough hands grab you and fling a sack over your head. When you kick and yell at your captor, you're clonked on the head for your trouble, and darkness descends.

**Go to page 116.**

Y ou and Scarlett scramble your way down a dusty, cobwebbed passage. Soon you have the choice between heading down a shaft (there are iron rungs set into the wall and they don't look very sturdy!) or continuing the way you're going.

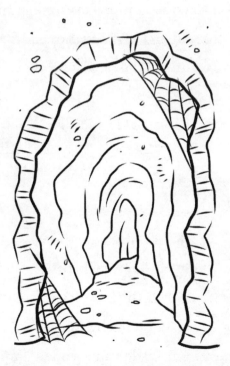

To keep going, head to page 102.

To climb down the shaft, head to page 21.

G uy yells at you to leave the knight alone – you can't hope to win against a foe in armour, who looks to be twice your size! – but you charge up to the knight anyway. It pulls back its visor to reveal the smirking face of Pedro Silva. There's unmistakeable malice in his eyes as he says, 'What a shame you decided to come up here, to these slippery battlements. Such an unsafe place for a young person to go running around!'

Before you can tackle him, he swings his huge mace. Next thing you know, you've been whumped through the air like a tennis ball. You go flying over the castle wall and plummet down towards the green forest below. It looks like it should be soft and fluffy to land on, and you know what they say – seeing is believing. Except in this case it's just not true. Your landing is spiky. And scratchy. And, most importantly, fatal. Shame your castle caper ended almost as soon as it began!

**RUN AGAIN?** TURN TO PAGE **8**

# 100

The moment you try to climb back up the shaft, a hidden mechanism springs into life. An iron grating slides across the shaft, closing it off completely. Scarlett curses. There must be some cunning system of weights and measures that can tell how much gold you've taken! The skeleton's jaw falls open as if it's laughing. You're going to be stuck here for a very long time ...

HAHAHAHAHAHAHAHA

RUN AGAIN? TURN TO PAGE 8

You head off to rejoin Scarlett. But on your way there, you tread on a mysterious-looking panel in the floor that is engraved with intricate shell patterns. Immediately a trapdoor opens beneath you and you're shot straight into an underground corridor.

Before you can yell for help, the trapdoor closes above you. There's only one thing for it. Start walking and hope you stumble upon a way out . . .

Go to page 36.

Y ou hear voices as you edge along the secret passage. It's Pedro Silva and his gang. They're on the other side of this wall, and they're discussing you! Pedro seems to think his team will be able to win by cheating. They've figured out how to set many of the castle traps off, and they are going to take you out of the game, but in such a way that it looks like an accident.

Scarlett is enraged – she's not having that! – and comes up with an idea. She'll stay close to Silva's team, spying on them and spoiling their plans, so that you can explore safely. Meanwhile, you can head off on your own and search for the Golden Idol. It's a fantastic plan, especially since Scarlett might be able to snare Silva in one of his own traps.

Scarlett sneaks off to sabotage the saboteurs, while you head deeper into the maze of secret passageways.

Eventually you find yourself in the damp rough-hewn corridors below the castle.

**Head to page 36.**

You manage to hook the bellrope and pull it over to the ledge. You wrap your arms and legs around the rope, cling on for dear life and slowly lower yourself down. Your weight swings the clapper and the bell clangs so loudly that it very nearly bursts your eardrums. The things you'll do to win a treasure hunt!

'Careful,' Guy warns.

'This was your idea!' you remind him.

You don't look down. There's a giddying drop below you that might give you vertigo. Instead, you grip tightly on to the rope and pull yourself up a few feet, inside the bell itself.

You shine your little spotlight torch around the bell's hollow metal interior, and grin at what you see. Guy's instincts have led you right. Dangling inside is a glistening pearl!

It's the size of a mango, strung on a fine silken rope. What a crazy place to hide something so valuable! You cut the rope and carefully tuck the pearl into your treasure sack.

Note this down in your Treasure Hunter's Log: **Giant Pearl.**

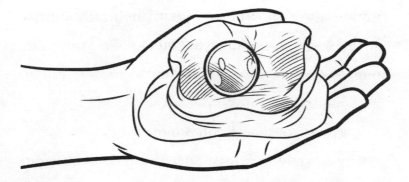

As you dangle with your priceless treasure, it occurs to you that this might be a good time to press the GAME OVER button, and stop the treasure hunt before you get into any more danger.

---

To press the button, head to page 145.

To try to get back to the battlements, where the knight is waiting for you, and search for more goodies, head to page 143.

You run and go into a skid. You cleverly zoom past the open ovens, and the blasts of flame roar over your head. But the floor is too greasy for you to stop! You keep skidding, out of control, towards a very unpleasant looking set of stone steps at the back of the kitchen. You bounce down the them one by one and end up buried in the rotting garbage the castle cooks throw out.

For you, the treasure hunt is over. You have a very long shower to look forward to. Sadly, without your help, your team fails miserably and Pedro Silva has his revenge. What a rubbish ending . . .

**RUN AGAIN?** TURN TO PAGE **8**

You stagger down the stairs, but you're just not fast enough. The banister would have been quicker; Francisco's already zooming down it to freedom. The Winged Screamers flock all over you, clinging to your hair and face. You expect them to eat you alive, but it seems they just want to hang on to you and scream. And the more you try to brush them off, the tighter they cling on! You can't hunt for treasure with that din in your ears.

You have to go back upstairs and hunt for ear plugs, while your team does the best they can without you. Sadly, their best isn't good enough, and you lose. But at least you've got some new pets out of the experience. Clingy, shrieky, nibbly pets that never leave you alone, sure, but they're kinda cute once you get to know them.

EEEEEEEEEEEEEEEEEEEEEHH!

RUN AGAIN? TURN TO PAGE 8

The two of you whizz down the banister and are pitched into a dingy, dungeon-like corridor. Francisco hurriedly bolts the door behind you just in case the Winged Screamers catch up. You have the choice of a door to your left, with a picture of a skull and crossbones on it; a door to your right, with a picture of a coin on it; or a door straight ahead, with a picture of a helmet on it.

Skull and crossbones door? Head to page 109.

Coin door? Head to page 110.

Helmet door? Head to page 33.

You rifle through the trophy cabinet, but nothing here seems to be worth calling 'treasure'. It's just rubbish golfing trophies made of brass, and sad-looking cups that haven't been polished in years.

'Found anything?' Scarlett says.

'No. It's all just junk.'

'So much for that guide I downloaded. I guess billiard tables and animal heads were what folk thought was "interesting" back in Victorian times.' Let's try somewhere else − I've already got a good idea of where.'

Just as you're wondering if the cabinet has a false bottom you could pry open, the eyes on the creepy portrait move.

'Scarlett? I think we're being watched.'

'You're right.' Scarlett's already backing towards the door. 'Let's get out of here. Coming?'

---

**To run out of the room like Scarlett wants, head to page 82.**

**To wait and see, head to page 73.**

You were worried this door might lead to CERTAIN DEATH, but it doesn't. It's some kind of laboratory — that's what the symbol on the door meant. The walls are lined with chemical flasks.

Francisco's eyes grow wide. 'This is an alchemist's lab! Whoever worked here was looking for the ultimate prize. The secret of turning base metals like iron and lead into gold!'

He's determined to try. Surely no amount of treasure can compete with the ability to make as much gold as you want? (Francisco, you realise, is seriously into gold. In an unhealthy kind of a way.)

---

**To help him with his experiments, head to page 113.**

**To pretend to help but mess up the experiment on purpose so he'll give up and get on with the treasure hunt, head to page 114.**

**To leave Francisco to his alchemy and slip off on your own, head to page 36.**

Francisco squeals with glee when you fling the door open and reveal a room with several huge chests against the walls. But his squeal turns into a wail of despair when he flings the chests open to find they have been emptied already. Only a few coins and trinkets remain.

'Pedro Silva!' he hisses. 'That cur. He has beaten me to the treasure room!'

You gather up what scraps of treasure you can find. You notice something Francisco hasn't spotted – a ruby shard ring that's rolled away into a crack in the flagstones.

**Note this down in your Treasure Hunter's Log: Ruby Shard Ring.**

'This cannot be all there was,' Francisco mutters. 'Perhaps it is meant to be a bluff. Yes. A trick! That must be it. There must be a real treasure room here somewhere. I can still find it! Ha ha ha!'

'Shouldn't we be looking for the Golden Idol?' you say.

'Pah. The idol is just a legend. It probably isn't even real. Not like real gold. I can smell gold, you know. This nose of mine? It is magical.' He taps it and smiles proudly.

Francisco seems more than a little crazy as he searches the walls and floor, trying desperately to find a hidden doorway somewhere. You decide to leave him and his magic nose to it. You slip away while he's busy, wondering what's behind the other doors.

But you never find out. When you go back through the door, you come out into a corridor you've never seen before. How is that even possible?! You press on, sure you'll see something you recognise any minute.

It's at least an hour before you admit to yourself that you're well and truly lost.

Head to page 36.

You grub around in the soil by the flytrap, hoping to uncover the Golden Idol, or some jewels, or maybe a solid silver watering can or something. No such luck. Your spade turns up a load of delicate-looking roots that you think must be the giant flytrap's feet.

There's a crash of thunder and the door vibrates. Or did something just bash it?

'Maybe we ought to leave,' Guy warns.

You bend down and gently feel around the roots, just in case there are any coins or anything down there. A shudder goes through the giant flytrap. What was that?

To ignore the shudder and carry on feeling the roots, head to page 115.

To cut your losses and run on to the next tower, head to page 27.

To your amazement, Francisco's experiments seem to be successful. He transforms an old tin kettle into what looks like solid gold.

**Note this down in your Tresure Hunter's Log: Golden Kettle.**

So what if Francisco transformed it? It's treasure, and you 'found' it in the castle, so it still counts!

Unfortunately, the second attempt doesn't work. Nor does the third. Francisco's obsessed with figuring out what he did right the first time. You'll never be able to drag him out of here now.

---

If you want to press the GAME OVER button and end the treasure hunt, head to page 145.

If you want to quietly leave the lab through the far door and explore on your own, head to page 36.

# 114

You sneakily slip a pinch of the wrong coloured powder into one of Francisco's flasks when he's not looking. You expect it to fizzle. Instead, it explodes with such force that the entire castle shakes. There's nothing left of either of you but a wisp of smoke. Oh well. If the castle wasn't haunted before, it certainly is now — by the ghosts of a careless young treasure hunter and a very grumpy Spaniard. How are you at rattling chains and groaning?

**RUN AGAIN?** TURN TO PAGE **8**

Y ou keep on running your fingers over the roots. The giant flytrap shudders some more and a funny squeaky noise comes out of it. Its limbs twitch. Suddenly, you realise it's laughing. Of course – the roots are its feet, and you're tickling them!

Encouraged, you tickle and tickle. The creature shakes and guffaws. It gapes its jaws wide, dropping the egg-like object it was holding. You quickly grab the egg and scrape the gunge off it.

This isn't just any old egg, you realise as a gleam of gold catches your eye. It's a bejewelled collector's item worth a huge amount of money.

**Add this treasure to your list: Jewelled Egg.**

You tuck it away in your collecting sack, glad to have scooped up such an amazing treasure . . . especially since nobody, animal or vegetable, got hurt.

You leave the giggling plant beast and head on to the next tower.

**Run on to page 27**.

You wake up in a pitch-black prison cell. From the cold stone walls around you, you guess you're somewhere below the castle. One wall is made of rusty old iron bars, with a door set into them. You give it a tug. Locked, of course. You were wondering how far Pedro Silva would go to sabotage you, and now you know.

And, worse, they have taken your treasure-hunting sack, and all its contents! What utter scoundrels. Now any treasure your team had collected up to this point will count for nothing. But you've no time to dwell on your bad luck. You need to escape, and fast.

A loose stone in the wall catches your eye. You tug at it, and pull it free. Cool air blows from the hole you've made. Encouraged, you pull out a few more until there's a hole big enough for you to crawl through. It's a tight squeeze, but you manage it. You find yourself in a corridor. At the end of it you glimpse a strange, shell-encrusted chamber.

**Head straight to page 117.**

Your heart beats fast as you walk down the corridor towards the archway before you. There's no sound except for the crunch of your footsteps on the rough rock. This deep underground, the silence is uncanny. You must be far, far beneath the castle. You don't know how far, but you guess you're at least as deep down below the ground as the tallest tower is above it.

You step through the stone arch and into the cold, echoing chamber beyond. The beam of your torch lights up walls encrusted with seashells, carvings and sculpted faces. It looks nothing like anything else you've seen in the castle. There are white fragments on the floor that might be bones. You don't look too closely at those.

Your mind drifts back to the legends you heard about the castle . . . legends of a secret underground temple where the fabled Golden Idol lies hidden. Could this bizarre room be that temple? You look around at the shell-covered pillars, wondering who built all this, and sudden excitement grips you as you see a glittering object at the centre of the room.

It's a golden idol, shaped like a little man pulling a face. You hardly dare to breathe. The legends were true. The idol really exists – and you've found it!

You reach out for it. But then you hesitate. Wasn't there another legend, something about a Beast? From what you remember, it was supposed to guard the idol.

You shrug. There's no Beast here, and nothing to stop you taking the treasure. This is your chance to win the treasure hunt and make yourself rich!

Now you just have to get it out of here. You grab the idol, and a bellowing roar shakes the room. You gulp. Looks like the Beast was real after all. Thumping footsteps shake the room, coming closer and closer. Any moment now, you'll find out what it really looks like. Great. You can tell Philip Appleton the truth, if you get out of here alive.

There's a crash and a boom. Fragments of flying rock rattle past your face. A monstrous creature like an enormous demon monkey with a skull for a head smashes its way through the wall and roars. It sees you. Huge claws reach out.

There's only one thing to do, and you do it. You run for your life!

You spot an exit. It's another archway, bigger than the first. You tuck the idol under your arm and sprint towards it. The demon monkey comes stampeding after you. It smashes the rock pillars and tramples the bones underfoot, and it doesn't even slow down.

You run along the tunnel, gasping, until it opens

out into a chamber where luminous mushrooms glow, lighting up the walls and floor with ghostly pools of light. There are three ways out of here, and a decayed old wooden sign on the wall tells you where they lead.

You can run up a steep winding staircase, which the sign says is TO THE BATTLEMENTS. You can charge through a set of double doors, which will take you TO THE GREAT HALL. Or you can follow the tunnel straight ahead, TO THE CATACOMBS. Whichever route you choose, you know the demon monkey will be right behind you!

**To run to the battlements, run to page 121.**

**To run to the great hall, run to page 130.**

**To head to the catacombs, run to page 136.**

You run up the steep winding staircase. Your legs ache. This is hard work! From behind you comes the heavy panting of the gigantic demon monkey as it squeezes itself into the narrow stairway. You hope it gets stuck. That would buy you valuable time to escape.

At the top of the stairs is an old-fashioned elevator cage with a sliding metal grille across the front. You press the 'call elevator' button about a hundred times. Stupid thing, why won't it hurry up? At least it's still working. You can hear machinery creak and groan from up above.

You can't see the demon monkey yet, but you can still hear it struggling up the stairs. The idol feels heavy in your hand. Maybe you should give it back? No, you decide, that probably wouldn't help now.

Finally, the elevator carriage comes sliding into view, just as the demon monkey's colossal claw reaches around the curving stairs for you. You yank the grille open, climb inside and slam it shut behind you. The demon monkey's hideous skull-face appears. It lunges at the grille, snapping its jaws, scraping its teeth against the metal. You desperately push a button, but which one?

To press the topmost button,
head up to page 123.

To press the bottommost button,
head down to page 86.

The carriage lurches up the shaft. You hear the demon monkey's angry bellowing echo from below. It's not happy that its prey is escaping! You lean against the carriage wall and relax. Now might be a really good time to press the GAME OVER button.

Just as you're about to push it, there's a loud *clanggg* and the carriage slows down. Something very heavy has caught hold of the underside of the elevator. No prizes for guessing what it is!

The elevator creaks, shudders and groans right to the very top. You haul the grille open and look out at the castle battlements. Rain is pouring down, washing over the stone walkways and dripping from a very surprised Guy Dangerous, who's looking right at you.

'Where the heck have you been?' he shouts. You notice there are cobwebs in his hair.

There's no time to explain. 'M-M-MONKEY!' you yell, and run past him. Guy sees the demon monkey come climbing out of the elevator shaft behind you and he promptly runs up to your side.

Together, the two of you run along the rain-slick castle battlements with a very angry demon monkey chasing you. You leap over piles of rubble and dodge around gaping holes in the pathway that would send you plunging into the moat if you fell into them.

'We've got to shake this thing off!' you gasp. 'Any bright ideas?'

'Only one, and it's a long shot,' Guy says. 'See that sharp corner up ahead? If we stop there and let the demon monkey charge us, then dodge at the last minute . . .'

'. . . then it might fall over the edge,' you finish. 'It's gotta be worth a try.'

'Let's do this!'

You run up to the corner, where the battlements twist around to the right, and turn to face the oncoming demon monkey. With trembling hands, you hold up the idol. 'This what you're after, huh?'

The demon monkey screeches in fury and puts on a burst of speed. It's a terrifying sight as it runs right up to you. You wait until the very last second to dodge, but which way should you go?

---

To lunge sideways and hope the demon monkey skids past you, head to page 39.

To drop down and hope the demon monkey soars over you, head to page 128.

You ignore Guy's advice and slide down to the guttering. It's ancient and packed with moss. This castle must leak like anything in winter. You rest your feet on the gutter and start to cross the distance, leaning in against the tiles. It's all going brilliantly until the gutter breaks.

You grab on for dear life. Directly below you, you see an open pipe mouth, the top of a huge stone drainpipe. It looks wide enough for you to fit into it. Apart from being made of stone, it's a lot like a water flume at the swimming pool.

You need to decide what to do quickly. If you let go now, you'd drop right into the pipe. You wouldn't have to worry about falling to your death, but heaven alone knows where you'd end up.

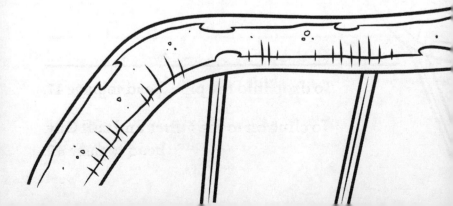

You'd have to be pretty desperate to ride a medieval water slide, but who knows? It might even be fun.

Or you could hang on to the gutter and yell for Guy to come and rescue you. He might be able to lift you back up on to the roof. That way, you wouldn't have to risk the pipe.

To drop into the pipe, head to page 47.

To cling on to the gutter and call Guy, head to page 49.

As the terrifying demon monkey lumbers towards you, you throw yourself at the floor. You glimpse its hairy body flying past overhead, and huge paws reaching for the idol in your hands. One claw gets a grip and tugs. The idol tumbles from your grasp and plops over the parapet.

There's a strangely sad-sounding howl as the demon monkey topples straight off the castle battlements with it and begins to plunge hundreds of feet downwards. Straight into the moat.

**RRROAAARRR**

You don't see the demon monkey hit the water, but you do hear it. It sounds something like **SPLADoOF.**

Guy flinches back from the parapet as the spray goes up.

You stand up and join Guy. Together you look down at the foam and spreading ripples.

'Did we get it?' you wonder aloud.

Guy slowly nods. 'I don't think it's coming back up. Whatever that thing is, it can't swim too good.'

You can hardly believe it. You've escaped from the Beast of Castle Gloomgarret, but you've lost the Golden Idol. Your relief at being alive makes up for your disappointment.

'Only one thing left to do,' you grin ruefully. 'GAME OVER!' And you press the big red button that ends the treasure hunt.

Turn to page 145.

You push through the double doors and run up a long flight of stairs. Flaming candelabras light your way. (You wonder who keeps replacing all those candles.) The demon monkey comes loping after you on all fours, squeezing its huge body through the doorway. It snorts and snuffles, as if it can smell you out wherever you try to hide.

At the top of the stairs is a carpeted corridor with portraits of ugly people from different eras of history. You race down it towards a bright light at the end. You're starting to wonder if you should have left the idol well alone. Winning a treasure hunt isn't as important as staying alive!

You run all the way to the end of the corridor and burst through into the great hall. You can hear the monkey's claws tearing up the carpet behind you as it runs.

The great hall is a huge room with a table the length of a tennis court. Chairs like wooden thrones have been set round it, and a roaring fire lights the whole place up, casting flickering shadows into the far corners. Up on the walls are crossed swords and axes. Sat at the throne at the end of the table, enjoying a salad and a glass of fizz, is Scarlett Fox.

'Snack break,' she explains. She frowns as she sees how exhausted and wild-eyed you look. 'Um . . . is everything OK?'

'NoeverythingisnotOKIfoundtheidolandIambeingchasedbyademonmonkeyHELP!' you manage to blurt out.

Scarlett looks doubtful for a moment, but the monstrous roar from the corridor behind you soon changes her mind. 'The Beast of Castle Gloomgarret!' she whispers.

'YOU THINK?'

Scarlett snaps into action. 'This way!' She grabs you by the hand and runs from the room, down yet another of the castle's many corridors. The demon monkey scrabbles into the great hall, stops, sniffs the air and comes bounding after you again.

'What's the plan?' you gasp.

'I'm making it up as I go along,' Scarlett replies. 'We've got to lose that big ugly brute somehow. I've been looking over some plans of the castle, and I think there's a way.'

As you run, Scarlett explains her plan. The castle's music room was built right above a deep cellar, and it has a disused trapdoor in the middle. 'If I can get that trapdoor open, you can lead the demon monkey into it, and bingo!'

'You make it sound so easy!' you say with heavy sarcasm.

'You got a better idea?'

Unfortunately, you don't. Scarlett tells you which way to run to get to the music room, and runs off down a secret passage to get there before you. You lead the demon monkey on a merry chase up staircases and down again, through galleries and in and out of stately bedrooms, until you think Scarlett's had enough time to set the trap.

You find the music room where Scarlett said it would be. There's a grand piano, an expensive-looking violin, and a brand new electric guitar. There's also a large square rug looking suspicious in the dead centre of the room.

Now's your chance. You can stick to Scarlett's plan and lead the demon monkey on to the trapdoor. But just as you're about to, you realise you're right by the main castle gateway and the door is open.

You don't have to go through with this dangerous plan of Scarlett's. You could just pelt straight out of the castle with the idol and keep on running. For all you know, Scarlett hasn't even managed to set the trap up. You can't see her anywhere!

---

To stick to the plan and try to lead the demon monkey over the rug, head to page 134.

To run from the castle into the countryside, head to page 57.

'This had better work,' you mutter to yourself. You run toward the rug, jump straight over it and skid on the varnished floor.

The demon monkey is right behind you. Then, suddenly, it's not. Like a magic trick, the monster vanishes before your eyes, taking the rug with it. Both demon monkey and rug have plunged through the wide-open trapdoor that was hidden beneath it, just like Scarlett said.

Scarlett comes running from behind the curtain where she was hiding. 'Quick! The piano!'

'What?' you boggle.

'We need to barricade it in there. Hurry!'

You and Scarlett haul the piano over to the trapdoor, turn it over and leave it blocking the opening. The demon monkey's mournful cries boom up through the floorboards. It pounds its fists, but can't escape. It's trapped down there, for now.

You gaze at the idol in your hands. You can't quite believe you really did it. You defeated the Beast of Gloomgarret and made it out with the priceless Golden Idol!

Scarlett interrupts your reverie. 'Team Captain,' she pants, 'would you be a dear, and end the treasure hunt? I don't know about you, but I, for one, have had quite enough!'

'My pleasure,' you tell her. With a flourish, you press the GAME OVER button. The hunt is at an end, and it's time to tot up the scores and find out who's won.

**Head to page 145.**

The catacombs turn out to be a maze of little cellars, thick with dust and webs. With nothing to light your way but your torch, you run from room to room, desperately looking for a way out.

The demon monkey just won't give up. Whenever you think you've shaken it off, it lumbers around the next corner behind you and you have to start running again. All the rooms down here look the same. It's like being trapped in a bad dream . . .

Then, just when you think you'll never get out, you hear a familiar voice. 'It's all mine! Come to me, you pretty, pretty things . . .'

Francisco Montoya! You run towards the sound of his voice. Francisco is standing over a lifted-up slab in the floor. In the hollow beneath is a metal chest brimming over with treasure: necklaces, bracelets, jewels and rings. Francisco's stuffing them into his pockets. He sees you clutching the idol, you see him, and suddenly he looks very guilty.

'I was, ah, collecting treasure for our team!' he says with a weak grin.

You're about to tell him that all the treasure's supposed to go in the treasure-hunting sack, not in his pockets, but just then the demon monkey barges into the room. It rears up and roars at you, sounding more furious than ever.

Francisco shrieks. 'Arghh! You've led the Beast of Gloomgarret right to me. Now it's after us both!'

'RUN!' you yell at him.

The pair of you sprint out of there, luckily ducking out of the way of a low stone arch. The demon monkey slams its head right into it, and while it staggers giddily for a moment, you and Francisco are able to get a head start running away.

'You should not have come to me,' Francisco grumbles, shedding gold and jewels from his pockets as he runs. 'The Beast is the guardian of the castle's treasure. It knows you have the idol. It will not stop until it catches us!'

'Well, some treasure hunt this turned out to be,' you gasp. 'How are we going to get this demon monkey off our backs?'

'We have two choices!' snaps Francisco. 'I recognise this part of the dungeons. Up ahead, there is an underground river. We could jump into it and swim for our lives. It probably leads out of the castle. The demon monkey may not be able to follow.'

'That sounds like a terrible plan. What's the other choice?'

'We make for the staircase. The long, rickety staircase back up to the castle. The demon monkey is heavy, yes? The stairs may not take its weight.'

'Two terrible plans. I'm impressed.'

'Choose!' Francisco yells. 'The beast is almost upon us!'

Both of Francisco's plans sound pretty awful, but you're going to have to pick one of them or you'll be trapped down here forever.

---

**To run and jump into the underground river Francisco described, head to page 139.**

**To head to the rickety stairs, run to page 141.**

'Let's take our chances in the underground river,' you say.

'As you wish.' Francisco leads you down a set of damp-looking stone steps into a cold, wide cavern. Sure enough, there's a river flowing by – and there's even a little boat tethered to a dock!

'Quick!' Francisco urges you. 'Into the boat!'

You see the fearsome shape of the demon monkey looming at the top of the steps. You quickly climb into the boat. But instead of joining you, Francisco shoves you away from the shore!

'Hey!' you yell as the boat drifts off downstream. 'What are you doing?'

'Saving your life,' Francisco says. 'I think I can keep our demon monkey friend busy and buy you some time. Good luck!'

That's the last you see of him. The boat is picking up speed, and passes under a stone arch and down a tunnel. You can only hope Francisco got away safely.

To your horror, a splashing sound from nearby tells you that the demon monkey hasn't given up. It's following you down the river. You paddle with your hands, trying to go as fast as you can.

It's a relief when you see daylight again. The boat glides out of a cavern a way away from Castle Gloomgarret. You leap out and wade to shore, knowing the monster chasing you is only moments behind. You're somewhere in the Irish countryside, clutching the idol, with a demon monkey chasing you, and all you can do is run.

**Head to page 57**.

'Let's try the stairs,' you tell Francisco.

'I was afraid you would say that,' he grumbles. 'This way!'

The demon monkey pursues you through a winding set of cellars before Francisco finds the right door and leads you up on to the wooden spiral staircase. The moment you put your weight on the first step, it makes a dreadful splintering noise. Rickety isn't the word. There's more woodworm than there is wood.

'Hurry!' Francisco urges you.

Too late to back out now! You run up the stairs, leaping up them two at a time, hoping all the while that you won't fall through them and break your neck. Francisco is right behind you, and the demon monkey is right behind him.

You've only gone a few steps when there's a crash from behind you and a terrible cry. You spin around to see the monster vanishing from sight, through the broken steps in the staircase. Francisco was right. The stairs have broken under its weight!

# 142

But the demon monkey has caught hold of Francisco's shirt, and is pulling him down with him. Now Francisco's hanging by his fingertips from the broken remains of a step. As the demon monkey plunges down into the dark with a long drawn-out howl, Francisco begs you to help him.

You haul the grateful treasure hunter back to safety. All the treasure that was in his pockets has gone. Francisco shudders. 'Perhaps it is for the best,' he says. 'That gold was bad luck, I think.'

'I've had enough of treasure hunting for one day,' you announce. 'Let's end the hunt.'

'You took the very words out of my mouth, *amigo*!'

With that, you tuck the precious golden idol under your arm and press the GAME OVER button. The treasure hunt is done.

---

**Head to page 145 to find out whether your team or Pedro Silva's team are the winners.**

Carefully, you and Guy shuffle along the rooftop back towards the knight. It laughs at you and gets ready to throw some more rocks.

You duck and a rock flies over your head.

'How are we going to get back up there with that jerk standing guard?' you ask Guy.

'We're gonna have to rush it!' Guy growls.

'Good idea. One knight can't hit us both at once, right?'

Guy pats your shoulder. 'Get ready. On my mark. One, two . . .'

Guy never gets as far as 'three'. There's a sudden crash. The knight goes toppling backward over the battlements and only just manages to haul itself back before it falls. There's a huge dent in its breastplate.

You and Guy look at one another and hurry across the roof to the battlements. Down below in the courtyard, Scarlett Fox is waving at you. She's standing beside a full-size replica of a medieval catapult. She must have knocked the knight off its armoured feet with a flung boulder!

'Thanks, Foxy!' yells Guy. 'I owe you one!'

'My pleasure. Now move before that tin can catches up with you!'

The knight is already heaving itself back on to the walkway. You and Guy rush ahead to the next tower.

**Head to page 41.**

You make your way back to the entrance hall where the treasure hunt first started. Philip Appleton's there already with the others, smiling at you. 'Congratulations are due for finishing the hunt at all,' he says. 'I admit, it turned out to be more dangerous than I expected.'

Guy, Scarlett and Francisco all glare at him. 'You ought to be arrested, you crazy old coot!' Guy yells. 'This castle is a darned deathtrap!'

'But you did have fun, I hope?' says Philip seriously.

Everyone looks at you for an answer. You grin. 'Aw, it was nothing I couldn't handle.'

Pedro Silva's team troop into the room, scowling at you. They all look like they've had a terrible time. One of them is soaked to the skin, another has singed hair and eyebrows, and Pedro himself has a black eye.

'So,' Pedro spits, 'you are still alive.'

'Surprised?' you say.

'I admit, I am impressed,' says Pedro. 'You are not the amateur I took you for. You have been a worthy opponent. But you are still going to lose.'

# 146

Scarlett laughs. 'You ought to be disqualified, Silva! We all know you've been cheating.'

'Don't make accusations you can't prove, Scarlett!' sneers Pedro.

Philip steps between the two teams and holds up his hands. 'Enough. We will settle this according to the rules. Team captains, please lay all the treasures you have collected on the table.'

Go through your list of collected treasures and count up how many you've found. Remember, if you found the Golden Idol, it counts as four treasures all by itself . . .

**If you've found fewer than three treasures, head on to page 147.**

**If you've found exactly four treasures, go to page 149.**

**If you've found five or more treasures, run to page 151.**

Philip looks at your collection of treasures, and then at Pedro's. 'Oh dear,' he sighs. 'I must say, it gives me no pleasure at all to declare that Mr Silva's team has won.'

Pedro's team begins clapping and whooping. 'In your face!' Pedro laughs. 'Easy!' He scoops all the treasure off the table and into his sack. Guy, Scarlett and Francisco all look sickened. You can't believe it. After all you went through . . . the bad guy won?

'You can't let him get away with this, Philip!' whispers Scarlett. 'He's a cheat and a liar and you know it!'

Philip sighs. 'I know he's no angel, Scarlett. But I'm sorry to say that your young captain simply did not collect as many treasures as he did.'

Pedro swaggers over to you. 'Hey, kid. No hard feelings, eh? This is for you.' He drops something into your pocket. You fish it out. It's a single penny.

'Thanks,' you say sarcastically.

'Hey, it could be worse. At least you're not leaving

empty-handed!' Pedro guffaws.

Philip takes your team aside. 'Perhaps you would all be my guests for dinner tonight? It's the least I can do to make up for what's happened.'

'What about us?' says the woman on Pedro's team. 'Don't we get dinner?'

'Go buy your own,' Philip says coldly. 'The contest is over. Leave my home right away, and don't come back.'

The rest of the evening is kind of fun, surprisingly. You end up eating toast and playing board games by the fire, and listening to Philip's stories of his days as a treasure hunter. By the time you go to bed, you've almost forgotten the disastrous treasure hunt. Almost. But not quite.

You can't help but wonder how your adventure might have turned out if you'd made different choices along the way . . .

RUN AGAIN? TURN TO PAGE 8

Philip looks from your treasure pile to Pedro Silva's and back again. He coughs. 'Well, this is awkward. It seems both teams have collected exactly the same number of treasures.'

Guy laughs in disbelief. 'You mean to say it's a draw?'

'A tie. A dead heat. A stalemate.'

'So who WINS?' yells Pedro.

'Nobody,' says Philip with a shrug. 'I suppose you'll have to share the winnings . . .'

Pedro is spittingly angry about this. 'Share my treasure? With this jumped-up little pipsqueak?' he rants, pointing to you. 'NEVER!'

'I think you'll find it's still *my* treasure,' says Philip coldly. 'And if that's how you feel, I think you should leave. Your manners leave a lot to be desired.'

Once Pedro's team have left, with many backward glances and scowls, Philip has tea brought in for you all, and you settle down for a well-earned rest.

Your own share of the treasure won't come to much once it's been divided between the two teams, but you do get a cute little consolation prize – a miniature Golden Idol key ring made from real plastic! Oh well, at least it's a souvenir.

RUN AGAIN? TURN TO PAGE 8

Philip looks at Pedro Silva's pile of treasures, clicks his tongue disapprovingly, and turns to look at yours. It's obvious that your pile is more valuable by far. Pedro knows it, and so do Guy, Scarlett and Francisco. They're all grinning crazily. But Philip still makes sure to count every one of your treasures, out loud.

Then he shakes your hand. 'Congratulations, my young friend. You are the clear winner.'

Guy, Scarlett and Francisco cheer and clap. You can hardly believe it. You've made it through the craziest, deadliest treasure hunt ever, and you've won!

Pedro Silva's face slowly turns red. He slams his fist on the table. 'Unacceptable! They must have cheated!'

'Oh, one of the teams cheated all right,' says Scarlett. 'But it wasn't ours. It was yours.'

Pedro's mouth gapes for a moment, like a landed fish. Then he sticks out his jaw defiantly. 'Prove it.'

'OK.' Scarlett promptly holds out her hand to Philip Appleton and places a little USB drive into the retired treasure hunter's palm.

He looks impressed, but not surprised. 'Thank you, my dear. I see you have remembered what I taught you about surveillance.'

'You were a great teacher, sir,' Scarlett says with clear respect.

'Teacher?' you say. Scarlett just winks at you and mouths the words 'spy business'. Obviously there's a lot more to doddery old Philip Appleton than meets the eye.

'Silva,' Scarlett says, 'this drive holds spy camera footage of you and all of the members of your team cheating. On multiple occasions.'

Pedro blusters. 'I . . . er . . . we . . . that is . . .'

Appleton has hooked the USB up to Scarlett's tablet, and is watching the footage open-mouthed. 'Not to mention stealing,' he says in a voice of ice. 'You thought you'd pocket a few bits and pieces for yourself along the way, didn't you? Don't bother to deny it. Turn out your pockets, or I shall have you arrested.'

After Pedro Silva's gang have been kicked out of the castle, you settle down for a cosy evening with Philip Appleton and your winning team.

It starts with a seven-course banquet and ends with the best night's sleep you've ever had, in a huge four-poster bed covered with feather-soft pillows.

You'll be going home with riches you couldn't have dreamed of. Congratulations – you've won fair and square! But as you lie in bed, you can't help thinking that there's no way you you could have found all the treasures that Castle Gloomgarret has to offer. If only you could have another go, and see what secrets you could uncover next time!

**RUN AGAIN?** TURN TO PAGE **8**

# TREASURE HUNT LOG

Use this page to make a note of all the
treasures you collect on your hunt! Remember,
the Golden Idol counts as four treasures.

.......................................................................................
.......................................................................................
.......................................................................................
.......................................................................................
.......................................................................................
.......................................................................................
.......................................................................................
.......................................................................................
.......................................................................................
.......................................................................................
.......................................................................................
.......................................................................................
.......................................................................................
.......................................................................................
.......................................................................................
.......................................................................................
.......................................................................................
.......................................................................................